Little White Duck

Music by **Bernard Zaritsky**   Words by **Walt Barrows**   Illustrated by **Polly Powell**

There's a little white duck
    sitting in the water,
A little white duck
    doing what he ought-er;

He took a bite of a lily pad,
Flapped his wings
     and he said, "I'm glad

I'm a little white duck
    sitting in the water.
Quack! Quack! Quack!"

There's a little green frog
    swimming in the water,
A little green frog
    doing what he ought-er;

He jumped right off
    of the lily pad,
That the little duck bit
    and he said, "I'm glad

I'm a little green frog
    swimming in the water.
Glug! Glug! Glug!"

There's a little black bug
    floating on the water,
A little black bug
    doing what he ought-er;

He tickled the frog
   on the lily pad,
That the little duck bit
   and he said, "I'm glad

I'm a little black bug
    floating on the water.
Bzz! Bzz! Bzz!"

There's a little red snake
    playing in the water,
A little red snake
    doing what he ought-er;

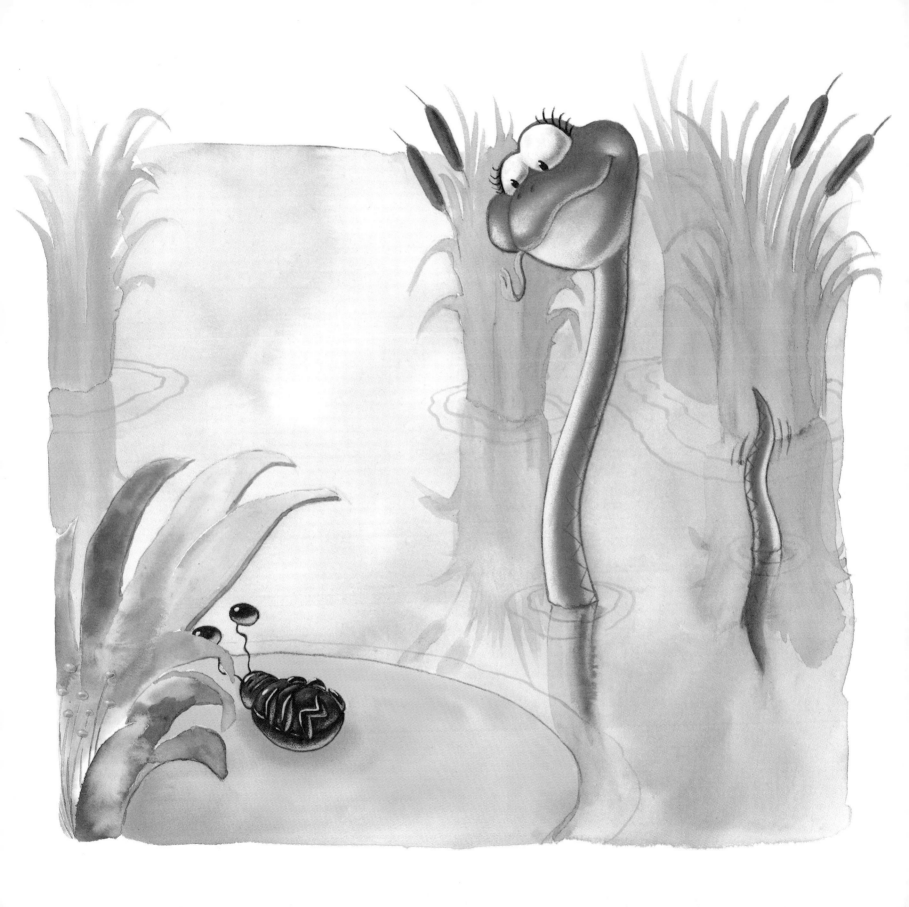

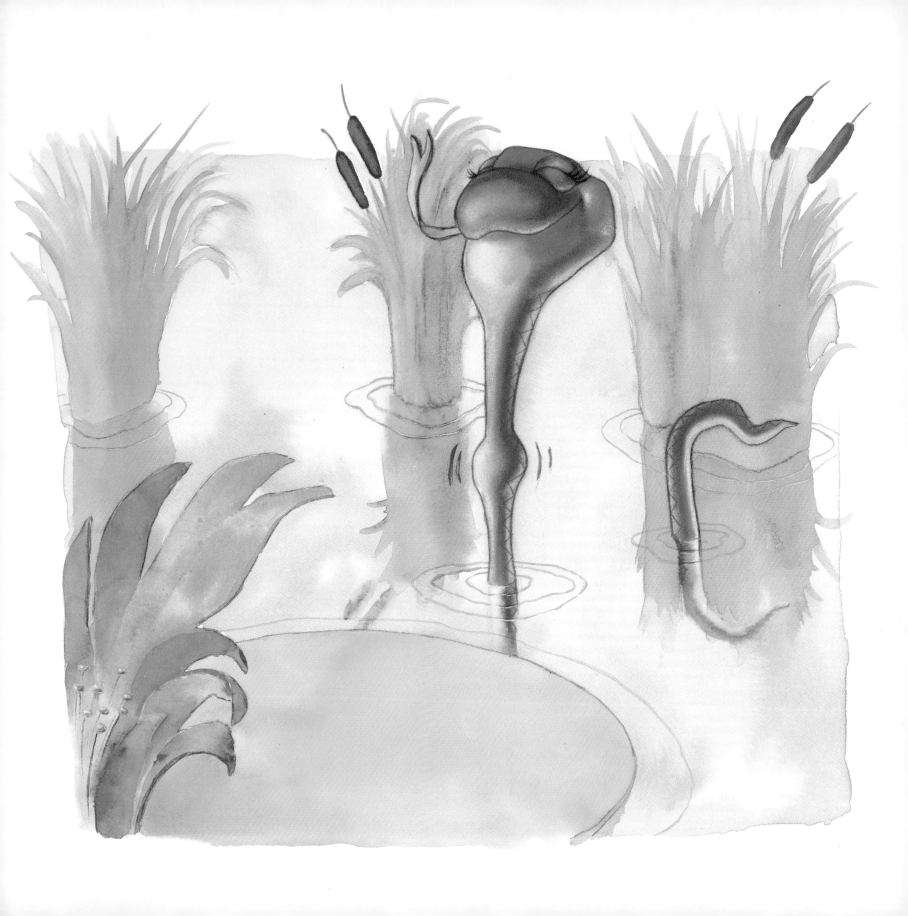

He frightened the duck
    and the frog so bad,
He ate the bug
    and he said, "I'm glad

I'm a little red snake
    playing in the water.
Hiss! Hiss! Hiss!"

Now there's nobody left
    sitting in the water,
Nobody left
    doing what he ought-er;

There's nothing left
but the lily pad;
The duck and the frog
ran away; I'm sad

'Cause there's nobody left
sitting in the water.
Boo! Hoo! Hoo!

Requests for permission to make copies of any part
of the work should be mailed to: Permissions
Department, Harcourt Brace & Company,
6th Floor, Orlando, Florida 32887

Grateful acknowledgment is made to SCREEN
GEMS-EMI MUSIC INC. for permission to reprint
"Little White Duck" by Walt Barrows and Bernard
Zaritsky. Song copyright © 1950 by COLGEMS-EMI
MUSIC INC.; song copyright renewed 1977 by
COLGEMS-EMI MUSIC INC.

Printed in the United States of America

ISBN 0-15-300402-9

6 7 8 9 10   035   97 96 95